The Twelve Days of Christmas

ILLUSTRATED BY JOHN O'BRIEN

Boyds Mills Press

For Tess

Publisher Cataloging-in-Publication Data
Main entry under title.
   The twelve days of Christmas/illustrated by John O'Brien.—1st ed.
[32]p. :col. ill. ; cm
Summary: Humorously illustrated edition of the traditional song.
HC ISBN 1-56397-142-9   PB ISBN 1-59078-086-8
1. Christmas music—Juvenile literature. [1. Christmas music.]
1. O'Brien, John, ill. II. Title.
783—dc20   1993
Library of Congress Catalog Card Number 92-73990   CIP

Published by Boyds Mills Press, Inc.
A Highlights Company
815 Church Street
Honesdale, Pennsylvania 18431
Printed in China

First edition, 1993
First Boyds Mills Press paperback edition, 2003
The text of this book is set in 14-point Galliard.
The illustrations are done in pen and ink, dyes, and watercol

10 9 8 7 6 5 4 3 2 HC
10 9 8 7 6 5 4 3 2 1 PB

On the first day of Christmas,
my true love gave to me...

A partridge in a pear tree.

On the second day of Christmas, my true love gave to me...

Two turtle doves

and a partridge in a pear tree.

On the third day of Christmas, my true love gave to me...

Three French hens,

two turtle doves,
and a partridge in a pear tree.

On the fourth day of Christmas,
my true love gave to me...

Four calling birds,

three French hens,
two turtle doves,
and a partridge in a pear tree.

On the fifth day of Christmas, my true love gave to me...

four calling birds,
three French hens,
two turtle doves,
and a partridge in a pear tree.

On the sixth day of Christmas, my true love gave to me...

Six geese a-laying,

five golden rings,
four calling birds,
three French hens,
two turtle doves,
and a partridge in a pear tree.

On the seventh day of Christmas,
my true love gave to me...

Seven swans a-swimming,

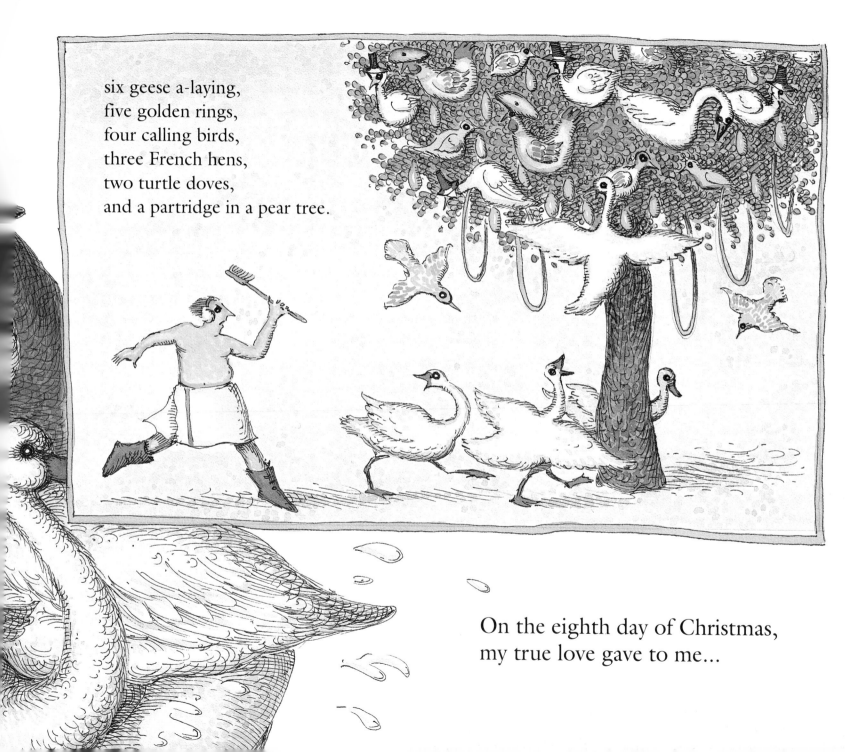

six geese a-laying,
five golden rings,
four calling birds,
three French hens,
two turtle doves,
and a partridge in a pear tree.

On the eighth day of Christmas,
my true love gave to me...

Eight maids a-milking,

seven swans a-swimming,
six geese a-laying,
five golden rings,
four calling birds,
three French hens,
two turtle doves,
and a partridge in a pear tree.

On the ninth day of Christmas,
my true love gave to me...

Nine ladies waiting,

eight maids a-milking,
seven swans a-swimming,
six geese a-laying,
five golden rings,
four calling birds,
three French hens,
two turtle doves,
and a partridge in a pear tree.

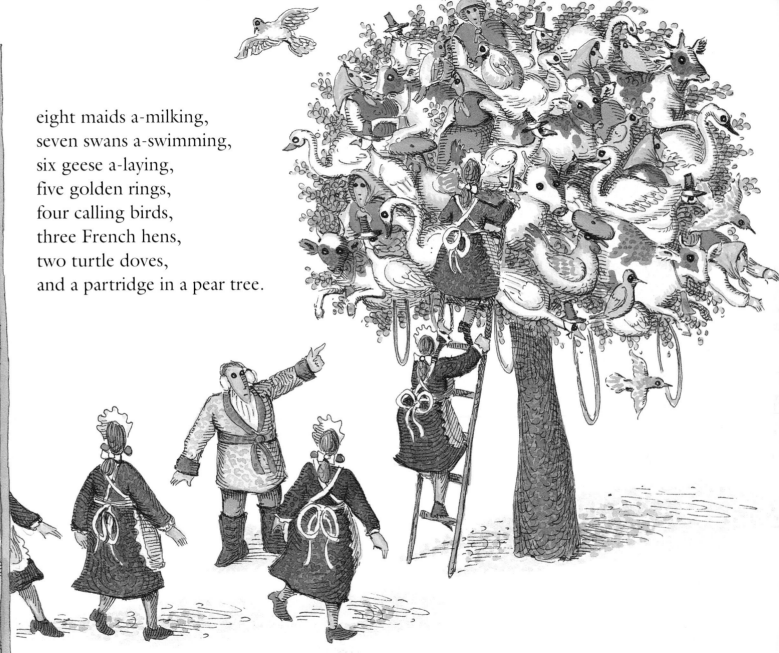

On the tenth day of Christmas, my true love gave to me...

Ten lords a-leaping...

nine ladies waiting,
eight maids a-milking,
seven swans a-swimming,
six geese a-laying,
five golden rings,
four calling birds,
three French hens,
two turtle doves,
and a partridge in a pear tree.

On the eleventh day of Christmas, my true love gave to me...

Eleven pipers piping,

ten lords a-leaping,
nine ladies waiting,
eight maids a-milking,
seven swans a-swimming,
six geese a-laying,
five golden rings,
four calling birds,
three French hens,
two turtle doves,
and a partridge in a pear tree.

On the twelfth day of Christmas,
my true love gave to me...

Twelve drummers drumming,

eleven pipers piping,
ten lords a-leaping,
nine ladies waiting,
eight maids a-milking,
seven swans a-swimming,
six geese a-laying,
five golden rings,
four calling birds,
three French hens,
two turtle doves,

and a partridge in a pear tree.